The Easter Cat

The Easter Cat

by Meindert DeJong

Illustrated by Lillian Hoban

Aladdin Paperbacks

Aladdin Paperbacks
An imprint of Simon & Schuster
Children's Publishing Division
1230 Avenue of the Americas
New York, NY 10020
Copyright © 1971 by Meindert DeJong
First Aladdin Paperbacks edition 1991

Printed in the United States of America

  5 6 7 8 9 10

Library of Congress Cataloging-in-Publication Data

DeJong, Meindert, 1910–
  The Easter cat/Meindert DeJong; illustrated by Lillian Hoban.—
1st Aladdin Books ed.
    p. cm.
  Summary: Although she has always wanted a cat, Millie is never
allowed to keep one until she finds one next to her Easter basket.
  ISBN 0-689-71468-8
  [1. Cats—Fiction.] I. Hoban, Lillian, ill. II. Title.
[PZ7.D3675Eas   1991]
[Fic]—dc20 90-24407 CIP AC

For Jan Crawford
and the lovely Ah So

Contents

MY CAT

But a cat is for keeping
A cat is a close thing
A cat is my own.

Frederick ten Hoor

The Easter Cat

chapter one

Mothers
in Alleys

Millicent stood in the alley, staring after her mother. She was disgusted with herself. Her mother had known the moment she'd seen her exactly why she was here. Always it was the same reason—to look for a stray kitten.

If she'd only waited! But she'd been so sure Mother had already left the house to go shopping, she'd hurried into her oldest jeans, had stopped in the kitchen just long enough to ram into her pockets two little plastic bags of leftover meat she'd teased off the T-bones of last night's dinner, then had dashed to the alley. All the time Mother must have been resting from the work of getting Easter dinner started for tomorrow. Then instead of properly going down the street, Mother had come down the alley.

Millicent stared after her in resentment. How could anyone have guessed? You don't think of mothers in alleys. All mothers have a thing about alleys—they think they're dangerous places. But where else could she find a stray kitten to feed and to play with?

Just like that Mother had come, and there she went now—of course only after making her promise she'd go back to the house. And, of course, Mother had seen the little plastic bags, with their red "twist-ems," popping out of her pockets. Why did they make pockets so small? Now Mother knew that she didn't only go to the alley to play with some kitten there, but that she even took things from the house to feed it.

Mother couldn't help it that she was allergic to cats and afraid of alleys, but couldn't she realize that the stray kittens in the alley needed to be fed? They were lost and scared and starved. It wasn't fair just to play with them—they had to be fed. They came to the alley's old warehouse to hunt for rats and mice, only to be chased and mauled by the big, fierce cats that already lived there—they never got enough to eat.

All the way up the alley back to the house Millicent thought it out long step by long step. She had a clear, right-worded thought with every step she took. She half turned as if to run and explain to Mother that if she couldn't have a cat of her own in the house because of Mother's allergy, she at least had to have the kittens of the alley to hold and to love and to play with and feed. But she didn't turn. All it would do would be to make Mother feel bad. Mother couldn't help it.

Millicent turned out of the alley at their own garage, crossed the yard, climbed the steps of their high, old-fashioned back porch, and sat down on the top step. She'd sit right here. Maybe she had promised not to play in the alley with kittens, but if one came . . . . She took out the little plastic bags, opened them, and set them on each side of her. Maybe the smell of the meat would bring a cat.

No kitten came. Millicent leaned back with her hands flat on the porch behind her and looked drearily around. The family never sat on this porch—there wasn't even a chair to sit on. On the whole long porch there was only the enormous, old-fashioned cabinet phonograph that had been made into a planter for

ivy. Over the years the ivy had draped itself down the whole front.

Somebody, sometime, had painted the phonograph the same battleship gray as the porch floor. Now it looked like a great ugly, square toadstool, as if it grew and mushroomed up out of the floor. It looked so awful that she'd once asked Mother why she kept it.

Mother had laughed. "It is pretty bad, isn't it? But believe me, at one time I thought it was wonderful."

Millicent had shuddered.

"I know," Mother had said, "but that was the fashion then—plants growing out of old coffee grinders, milk churns, or copper teakettles. I wanted something unusual too, and there was this old phonograph just standing out in the garage, so I asked your father to make it into a planter for me. He took off the top, lined the shelf with metal, cut off the legs, and there was my planter."

"Glug," Millicent had answered.

"Well, I thought it was pretty original. I was only sorry it wasn't one of the real old kind with a trumpet —ivy tumbling out of a long black trumpet!"

"Mother!"

"Seems crazy now, but it didn't then. Anyhow, the

ivy did well and still does, and no one sees the old phonograph out here. Besides, the inside of the cabinet makes a handy place for my garden tools." Mother had been silent a long moment, then she'd said thoughtfully, "To be honest, I guess it's really because lining that phonograph for me turned out to be your father's last project before he died."

Remembering her mother's words somehow made Millicent feel guilty. The ugly phonograph seemed to be accusing her of hardly remembering her father. But she'd been little more than a baby then, she defended herself. She hastily scrambled up. She'd go in the house. Anyhow, if she stayed here Sarah might come, and she didn't feel like playing. No cat had come to be fed, and there was only the silent, dreadful phonograph that seemed to want the afternoon to be lonely and moody. Sarah would be no help.

Sarah was the only other girl that lived near. She was two years younger than Millicent, but she acted and talked as old as her own grandmother. Mother was always telling her to be nice to Sarah because she was lonely. Well, who wasn't lonely? Millicent stared at the ugly phonograph.

Then down the quiet backyards somewhere a

screen door slapped shut. It had been so still, the sound was almost a gunshot. Was it Sarah? If it was, Sarah would come, and Sarah was hard to get rid of. She stuck. Millicent jumped up and ran to the phonograph, pushed the trailing dangles of ivy aside and opened the cabinet door. Inside were a couple of small sprinkling cans, gardening gloves, a spray gun, a trowel, and a box that had tumbled over and scattered fertilizer on everything. She hastily spread everything over the porch floor. It looked busy, and she began brushing at the spilled fertilizer inside the cabinet.

Nobody came—the screen door slap hadn't been Sarah. Millicent pulled back out of the cabinet, and somehow felt cheated. Now there was nothing but the long, empty afternoon . . . . Well, why not make a real job of it? Get soap and water and clean the inside of the cabinet for Mother? It'd be something to do.

The gray fertilizer lay swept up in a peaked pile on the white bottom of the phonograph. The rest of the cabinet was dark mahogany, and Millicent idly wondered why her father had nailed a new bottom of white painted boards in it. Mother's gardening tools weren't that heavy! Oh, she guessed she knew —the old bottom must have got wrecked when he took out the pigeonhole racks that held the records. But he'd sure used big nails for the new white bottom! And it was all so long ago the nail heads had rusted, so that now they looked almost like tiny copper coins against the white boards. Millicent made herself believe they were some kind of foreign coins, and poked her head far into the cabinet to look closer.

As she did, the ivy hanging over the opening caught the barrette in her hair and stripped it away. It fell, and slid down into the crack between the white bottom and the dark mahogany side of the cabinet.

She tried to pry the barrette out, but the crack was so narrow even her little finger was too thick. She grabbed the trowel and jabbed at the crack. Suddenly the whole white bottom pulled up with the trowel and the barrette fell away down under the porch. Why, the bottom was hinged at the back with concealed hinges! It was a little trap door! The nails were nothing but nail heads—they had been cut off so the bottom only looked solidly nailed.

Excitedly Millicent poked her head down through the opening to look under the porch, but it was too dark. Disappointed, she was about to give up when she caught sight of the faint sparkle of the barrette lying below in the dirt. She twisted around and farther back in the dimness made out a partition that must be there to keep the long porch floor from sagging in the middle. But what was that half-moon-shaped spot just above the ground in the middle of the partition? Was it a crawl hole? And was that faint daylight coming through the crawl hole from a room beyond? Was there a secret room under the porch?

Suddenly Millicent heard tiny click-clacking sounds right below her face, saw small movements as if her barrette were clicking and stirring. She poked her head down. No, bugs! Shiny, hard-shelled beetles were scuttling over the dry, dusty dirt down there. One of them must have crossed the barrette.

Shuddering with revulsion, Millicent jerked back out of the cabinet, and jumped to her feet. She had to get a flashlight, see what was really down there. It was all so strange—the hinged false bottom in the phonograph for a trap door, a crawl hole in a partition to a secret room beyond, if it was a room. Millicent shivered, but raced into the house for the flashlight.

chapter two

The Easy Window

Upstairs Millicent stood hesitating. She needed Carl's big flashlight, but she wasn't supposed to go into his room. Then down in the driveway Sarah's call came. The call ended her hesitation. She pushed the door open, grabbed the flashlight from Carl's night table, and ran down the hall, stopping only to snatch Mother's bathrobe hanging over the stair railing. She pulled it around her as she ran to her room, and to the window that looked down on the driveway. From behind the curtains she peered out.

There Sarah stood, eyes with their thick, horn-rimmed glasses turned up toward Millicent's window. Patiently Sarah called again. That was Sarah, Millicent thought darkly, she wouldn't raise her voice, but neither would she ever stop until she got an answer. Over and over Sarah called, "Millie, Millie, Mill-eee, Mill-eeeee."

As if she were calling a cow, Millicent thought. That was how it sounded, like calling a dull, tedious, stupid old cow! She oughtn't to answer—ought to let Sarah stand there and call until Mother got home.

Mother! Oh, no! There was all the garden stuff scattered over the porch, and the phonograph open. Sarah was so nosy, Millicent certainly didn't want her to find out about the secret place. With Sarah it would stay about as secret as the Statue of Liberty. She'd have to get rid of her fast.

Millicent opened the window and leaned out so Sarah would be sure to see her bathrobe. "Moo," she sang out. "What do you want, Sar-eeeeee?"

"Oh!" Sarah gave a startled little shriek. "Millie, how you scared me!" But she looked modestly pleased. "Imagine, you calling me that—that's what my grandma always calls me—Saree."

What was the use? You could never kid Sarah. Millicent waited, unable to think of anything more to say.

"Millie, you scared me so, here I almost forgot

what I came for . . . . May I borrow your jump rope?"

Sarah was acting kind of funny. Usually she just teased her to come out and play. "Of course, you can," Millicent said easily. Then to make sure Sarah wouldn't ask, she added, "Wish I could play, but Mother said to wash my hair while she was gone. . . . Wait, I'll look for the rope."

Sarah looked up, not believing a word. She had a funny, old-grandmother way of making you feel lying and guilty. "Oh, your mother's gone? Do you have a cat up in your room?"

"Nope," Millicent said promptly, "just an old cow."

Sarah didn't think that funny enough even for a smile. Instead she said in a pleased, smug voice, "Oh, I forgot to tell you, but the jump rope isn't only for me. There's a new girl just moved in down the block, and I'm going to play at her house."

Millicent leaned out of the window. "A new girl?" To her surprise she felt a sharp flick of jealousy.

"I think she's younger than I am," Sarah said.

"Oh?" Millicent at once lost interest.

"Just a little younger," Sarah said hastily. "But she's a lot like you. She's crazy about cats too. Isn't it funny, now *me*, they make me feel squirmy all over. Everybody at my house feels like that about cats—except Grandma."

"Is that so?" Millicent tried to act as if it didn't matter, but couldn't help wincing. Always it hurt her that there were people who didn't like cats. Mother, of course, had her allergy, but her big brothers didn't care for them at all. Men seemed to like dogs better.

Maybe it showed on her face what she was thinking, for Sarah said, "Mama says it's no wonder you go overboard for cats. Just your mother and a big, grown-up brother who goes to college to live with. And the way you came along so far behind your two brothers. Mama says having two bossy brothers like that would be worse than having two fathers." Sarah giggled. "I don't know how you could have two fathers!"

Millicent smiled down, but felt mean. She'd like to wipe that old-grandmother smile off Sarah's face. "Well," she said stiffly, "you live with your mother and a grandmother, and your sister is way older too. So what's the difference?"

"I don't know," Sarah said earnestly. "I don't know about living with men. But it's so about you, Mama said."

Loudly Millicent called down, "Wait, and I'll look for the jump rope."

She turned away from the window to search her room, but her mind was on Sarah's family and what they'd said, and it took moments before she remembered that when she'd been skipping rope up here last week, Carl had ordered her to the basement. He'd claimed he couldn't study with the whole house shaking apart around his ears. Funny, but now that Sarah had brought it up, she guessed Carl *was* bossy. When Dave was still home, he'd always been bossy too—but, well, more serious, polite-bossy. Carl wasn't ever polite, but he joked with her a lot, and then you didn't notice the bossiness so much.

Oh, but here she stood mooning, and Sarah down there and the phonograph open and the garden stuff scattered around. "Are you still there, Sarah?" she called out.

"Yes, I am, Millie," Sarah called back, her voice sweet with patience.

"I'm sorry. I was hunting," Millicent yelled back, "but then I remembered the rope is down in the basement. I'll get it and hand it to you from the basement door since you're right there."

The jump rope was still hanging over the back of a chair near the furnace. Millicent grabbed it up, then stopped. If she went to the door, Sarah might see that she had her jeans on under the robe, and she'd know the robe was just an excuse not to come out and play. Sarah was smart about things like that. Better throw the rope to her from a basement window.

Millicent clambered up on the workbench and opened the hinged window above it. "Sarah," she yelled, "here I am at the window." She tossed the rope out and let the window swing shut as if by accident. It bounced open again, and as Sarah ran up, Millicent hastily called, "I've got to hurry now, or I won't get my hair washed before Mother gets back." She reached out to latch the window.

"Wait, Mill-eee," Sarah yammered. "I've got something for you. It's for letting us play with your jump rope." With two fingers Sarah easily shoved the window open wider, peered nearsightedly down, and dropped something into Millicent's hand.

Even in the dimness of the basement the little thing sparkled. Millicent held it toward the light from the window. It was a small enamel pin in the shape of a blue cat with one tiny, silvery eye. Millicent made an exclamation of delight. "Oh, thank you, Sarah!" Then she hastily jumped down from the workbench.

Sarah still held the window open. "I sent for it for you," she said plaintively. "But, imagine, a *blue* cat! What won't they think of next?"

Clutching the bathrobe with one hand, Millicent leaned hard against the workbench and held the pin up against herself for Sarah to see. "It's beautiful, Sarah," she said. "Blue! Oh, that was nice of you. I'm going to put it on the minute I've got my hair washed and get dressed. . . . But I've got to run now. Mother could come any moment." She desperately felt that if Sarah kept hanging on, Mother would really come home. Then—tomorrow Easter— there wouldn't be any chance to explore. Mother was always home. "I've got to go now, Sarah," she said helplessly.

"The pin's for letting me and the new girl play with your rope," Sarah began again. "I had it in the house for two weeks, but . . . ."

Suddenly Millicent could stand it no longer. "What was that?" she broke in. "That isn't my mother at the front door?"

Sarah jumped back and started for the front of the house. The window softly swung shut. Millicent hurried up the stairs and waited behind the curtained basement door where she'd be out of sight. Now if Sarah would only go—really go!

But Sarah was back. Pushing the basement window open, she called out, "It wasn't your mother, Millie. It wasn't anyone."

Behind the door Millicent held her breath.

After a silence, Sarah said, "Millie, what are you going to have for Easter dinner? Mama says ham is too heavy, we're going to have goose."

Sarah was a goose herself if she thought she'd fall for that old trick.

The window swung down, and finally Sarah moved away.

Behind the door Millicent stood and listened. Sarah was tricky—was she still in the driveway? There was a long silence, then from outside came a strange, distant-sounding muffled cry. A cat—a kitten? No, it was more a faraway, smothered sound as of a baby crying. Now it had stopped—probably Sarah imitating a cat from behind her hand to trick her to come outside.

Standing so quiet made Millicent aware of the stillness in the house. It was actually a little scary. She thought of the metallic click-clacking scuttle of the hard-shelled beetles in the blackness under the porch. If there were bugs, wouldn't there be spiders? Maybe those huge wood spiders almost as big as baby mice. And mice! And all kinds of flat, squirmy, hairy things you might set your hand on, crawling along in the dirt. She shuddered. Should she let it go till another day? Toss the stuff back in the phonograph, and do it some other day?

No, if she was going to do it, it had to be now. Mother was so seldom gone. And it was afternoon—everything was bright outside. She'd take the beach blanket and spread it out, push it ahead of her, and crawl on that. Why, she'd have Carl's bright, powerful flashlight!

Upstairs in her room Millicent grabbed the flashlight, then turned to her clothes closet to get the beach blanket, but tripped on the long bathrobe and almost fell. Furious, she yanked it off and rummaged in the closet, guessing that the beach blanket would be stored with the summer things in boxes on the shelves.

At last she found the box that held the beach blanket, and tucked away under it, her old teddy bear and a long, narrow, silly-looking yellow tiger. So *here's* where Mother had put them. When she was little she'd never gone to bed without those two. Oh, but wouldn't they be fine to take down with her under the porch? There was no one to see her, and her own old baby things—wouldn't it be sort of a cozy comfort to have them with her?

The blanket over her shoulder, flashlight in hand, and tiger and teddy bear tucked high under one arm, Millicent hurried down the stairs. The grandfather clock in the hall bonged out four strokes. Millicent stopped. What if Mother should come now? What if she'd come home by way of the alley? There'd be the whole garden mess scattered over the porch, and the phonograph standing wide open. Millicent bit her lip. What if even Mother didn't know about the false bottom Father had made for a secret way to get under the porch? He'd made it just before he died, Mother had said. What if he had died without telling anyone, and nobody knew? Only she now, by accident. In the whole world only she to know.

Except for the clock's harsh ticking the whole house seemed to wait as she leaned on the stair rail. And even though the clock ticked the house seemed stiller than it ever had before—as still as the darkness waiting under the porch.

The clock ticked on. Suddenly Millicent straightened. She was being silly, scaring herself silly. She had the flashlight—she wouldn't be in the dark, and if she first threw her things down, she could go down after them. If she shoved the blanket with the tiger and the teddy bear out ahead of her, she'd feel safe. Why, she had the flashlight, and light made everything safe.

Kneeling before the phonograph on the back porch, Millicent took time to shine the flashlight after she dropped the beach blanket that she'd tried to make fall as full open as possible. The big light shone harshly on the dark, musty dirt floor, but rayed out enough for Millicent to see the half-moon-shaped opening in the bottom of the partition under the porch. So that was the way to get into the secret room. She did not look that way again, but hurriedly dropped the bright yellow tiger and the fuzzy, worn teddy bear so that they landed in the middle of the open blanket.

Now in the light she did not see a single scuttle of beetles or a movement of anything, but maybe whatever awful things lived in the dark melted away until darkness came over them again. Suddenly Millicent

felt something touching her knee outside the phonograph. It was Mother's spray gun. She grabbed it and
shook it at her ear. There was still plenty of spray
in it. Wasn't that lucky? Wouldn't it be wonderful
to have the spray gun waiting for her when she went
down? She dropped it through the opening.

She shone the flashlight again. The spray gun had
fallen beside the long, skinny tiger, who lay on his
side. But the teddy bear had landed in a sitting position against the tiger and sat head tilted back, black
shoe button eyes turned up as if waiting for her.

That moment there came a shuddering bang that
shook the house and the porch. Its suddenness scared
Millicent so, she dropped the flashlight. It clanged as
it hit the round cannister of the spray gun, bounced
up, fell down again, and went out.

What if the bulb had broken? There wasn't time
to think about it. It was Mother home, Millicent
knew. With her arms full of packages Mother hadn't
held on to the door, and it had banged against the
wall so it shook the house.

Millicent dropped the false bottom into its place,
tumbled the gardening things into the cabinet, and
with quick flicks of her hand tossed the dangles of
ivy down over the shut cabinet door, hoping they'd

look undisturbed and natural. She hurried to the kitchen, and locked the back door.

There was no sound downstairs. Mother must have gone straight to her room to change her clothes. Yes, there lay her packages tossed on the table in the entry hall. Millicent stole up the stairs, slid into her room, and closed the door.

The door safely closed, Millicent took a deep breath, then did a sudden little dance around both sides of her bed. Oh, everything had turned out well, everything had gone just right, except maybe the flashlight. Everything was done. She hadn't got under the porch, but maybe that was even better. Now she could get used to the thought. And tomorrow was Easter, and Sally would be here. She liked Sally, maybe she could tell her the secret. It would be hard not to tell. All day Easter there'd be the secret, knocking against her teeth. It'd be hard to keep her mouth closed. She'd wait and watch, see if it would be safe to tell Sally.

Millicent danced the length of the room again. Suddenly Mother called out from the hall, "Mimi, are you jumping rope in there again?"

Millicent danced to the door and flung it open. "No, just dancing because tomorrow is Easter.

Mother, what did you get me new for Easter?''

Halfway down the stairs Mother looked over her shoulder and smiled. "Nothing much. . . . Been a good girl?''

"Good as honey," Millicent said brightly, thinking of the teddy bear sitting with the bright tiger down under the dark porch. "Good as honey, sweet as a teddy bear! Mooooo.''

"You're mixed up in your zoology," Mother said. "That sounded like a cow to me, and I'm almost sure bears don't moo.''

Millicent laughed, and danced down after her mother.

chapter three

Olives
Are Eggs

Millicent sat up in bed, her heart pounding. Something had scared her awake. Something from the secret room under the porch? Then a wailing sound soared up through the open window from the driveway below. Oh, cats! Cats were fighting in the night —that's what had wakened her. Now there came the haunted moans of a young cat backing away from the fight. Then the other cat caught it. The young cat gave one terrified shriek; there came a bang as of a door or window slamming shut. After that it was silent.

Millicent jumped out of bed and ran to the window. It had sounded as if the young cat had been slammed against the basement door by the other cat. Maybe it was hurt! Millicent leaned far out of the window, over and over she softly called, "Kitty, kitty."

Nothing answered, nothing stirred, and she could see nothing in the blackness but a gleam of water on the cement driveway. Sometime in the night it must have rained hard.

At last she gave up calling. The cat was gone, but shaken by her scary awakening, Millicent didn't feel like going back to bed—not right away. She opened the door of her room and stole down the hallway, hoping she could see from the top of the stairs what time it was on the grandfather clock. As she passed Carl's room she could hear him snoring. It was a friendly, safe sound.

She leaned over the stair railing and looked down into the darkness of the living room, but the white dial of the big clock was a murky nothing sending out its heavy tick-tocks.

The living room was a flat pool of black, but as she kept staring down, the white trim of the brown polished stair separated itself from the dark. Then gradually the pieces of furniture began to take familiar shape. The scare of the sudden awakening began to fade away.

There was a scraping and a whirring, and the clock bonged out. Five o'clock! Why, it was Easter. Easter had begun. Then right now behind the post on the last tread of the stairs should stand her Easter basket. Millicent stooped and peered but she couldn't see, and she didn't take a single step toward the darkness below. Oh, it was the cat fight that had started it, but as she looked down into the blackness she knew that finding the secret room under the porch had made the whole house secret and scary. Even the Easter basket couldn't get her down there.

Now as she leaned on the stair rail Millicent smiled, remembering how the Easter basket had started. Mother'd been sick that year, and Dave and Carl had taken over. But they'd waited until the night before Easter and by then the stores were all but sold out of Easter eggs. Dave was a dental student, and he'd decided that since candy was bad for the teeth and the eggs were gone anyway, they'd get something shaped like eggs. They'd settled on monster olives. They'd found one slightly broken, hollow chocolate rabbit, so that and a fluffy toy kitten had sat in the basket on top of a nest of the big olives—both of their bottoms a bit soggy.

Millicent grinned as she remembered the shock of her first olive. She'd broken pieces off the chocolate rabbit and eaten until they were all gone, then, still greedy for more candy, she'd stuffed an olive into her mouth. Gah! She could still remember the strange taste and her disappointment, but by the time the huge olive was gone, she'd decided she liked the taste. Now if the basket waiting for her down there was full of candy eggs instead of olives, she'd be thoroughly disgusted.

In the midst of dreaming Millicent became aware that Carl's snores were louder. He sounded funny. She ought to tease him about it tomorrow—he was always teasing her! He was the one she counted on to take her part whenever she needed help. Dave was a lot older and he'd been away a long time while learning to be a dentist. Now he had his own office and his own home, because he'd married Sally while he was away. Their house was on her way to school and Sally had said to come over and eat lunch with her whenever she got tired of the school cafeteria. Sally was nice. It was sort of fun to have a big sister, but she didn't know Sally very well yet.

Goodness, just thinking about lunch had made her so hungry maybe she'd have to go down and get the basket after all.

She hesitated, then just as her foot touched the top step, Carl's snores stopped. It was as if he was sitting up in bed listening to something. Right then in the new silence from the dark living room came a sound like a gasp or a hastily cut-off yawn. Slowly Millicent drew her foot back, with both hands clutching the rail she listened. The sound was not repeated and in a moment Carl's snores started again. Now the secret room pushed everything else from Millicent's mind. Slowly she backed away from the stairs, afraid to turn away from whatever was down below. She could hear the little slur sounds her bare feet made as she slid them over the hall runner. It seemed hours before she backed up against Carl's door. Softly, silently she reached behind her and eased Carl's door open a crack. Now she'd be able to dash into his room if whatever had made the sound should come upstairs.

Backed against the crack of the opened door she stiffened in terror, for suddenly she could smell the earthy, musty odor of the secret room under the porch. She could not only smell the dead smell but seemed to see a huge, hairy hand pushing up the bottom of the phonograph and slowly, inch by frightful inch, oozing out of it and gliding soundlessly into the house. The Thing that lived under the porch was in the house!

Under her weight Carl's door inched open farther, then in weak relief she recognized the closed-in smell. Carl always slept with his windows shut and often he dropped his sweat-soaked tennis clothes on the floor of his closet. That was the smell! Relieved, Millicent eased the door shut and leaned against it. Always she was scaring herself silly! Now she remembered that when Mother couldn't sleep she often went down to lie on the couch in the living room until she got sleepy. Of course, it was Mother who had yawned.

Faint snoring noises started up in unison with Carl's heavy snores. But that was Mother! That was Mother in her own room. Then what was down there in the dark?

Millicent was too frightened to move. Her mind scuttled beetle-like back and forth as now she remembered she hadn't locked the basement window after Sarah left. The Thing must have come up from the porch and slid into the house through the basement window.

Right then the sound came floating up again. Millicent held her breath. The silence grew. Whatever was down there was listening to her. She mustn't breathe, she mustn't move. But at last she could hold her breath no longer and it came out in a harsh, gasping sound. Immediately from the dark depths came a small, questioning miauw.

A *cat!* It was a cat! A cat was down there—a kitten!

The questioning miauw came again, and Millicent snapped on the hall light and flew down the stairs. There, around the bend of the stairs, stood her Easter basket and there, right below it, sat a kitten! His big blue eyes looked up at her. With a croon coming out of her throat she sank down beside him and gathered him into her arms. Nuzzling her face in his soft fur was enough for the moment, but at last she held him away from her and gazed in unbelief. He had blue eyes! They glittered like jewels, and around his ears and his smudgy, smoky little face he was soft gray-blue. The rest of him, all but his tail and legs, was creamy white. "Oh, you're lovely," she whispered, but the little cat wiggled away from her clutch. She lunged for him but as she put her foot down she stepped on something sharp and gave a smothered yelp. The scared kitten streaked toward the kitchen.

Millicent sat down to dig out whatever was in her foot, and found it was a split, pointed olive pit. She felt around below the step and found a small pile of pits on the carpet. The kitten had taken the olives from the Easter basket and eaten them—had even eaten the insides out of the few pits that were split. A blue cat that ate olives!

She limped into the kitchen. The kitten was in the sink, his face turned up to the faucet. When Millicent came he uttered a plaintive miauw. Then in impatience because she didn't seem to know what he wanted he miauwed out in such a harsh, raucous voice she was afraid he'd wake the whole house. He wanted water, and he wanted it now! No wonder, all those olives! Millicent hurried across the kitchen to him.

"Oh, you're beautiful," she whispered. He only looked up at the faucet. She turned the water to the tiniest slow drip that couldn't possibly choke him. He opened his mouth and drank greedily.

"Blue, you're blue!" She could hardly believe it. "Blue Angel! That's your name—and you're mine."

The water dripping in the sink was like a baptism.

"Mine," she said again as she gathered him up, switched out the light and ran up the stairs to her room. As she let him down onto her bed he reached up with his faucet-moist lips and stroke-kissed her chin.

Millicent almost dissolved as she sank onto the bed with him. Down below, the grandfather clock bonged the half hour. Millicent did not hear it.

chapter four

Voice of an Angel

Nobody must know she had found the little cat, it would spoil the Easter surprise for all of them. Later, before anybody got up, she'd take him back to the living room. Ah, but he was a wonder! She sat looking at the tight-curled blue bundle of him in pure adoration. It still couldn't be believed that he was hers. It couldn't! Of all the stray kittens she'd fed and played with there'd never been one like this— blue and cream with blue eyes like jewels. Well, but Blue Angel wasn't a stray. He was royal! You'd never find *him* in an alley.

She lay back and stretched full length beside him. Everything was unbelievably good now. The morning that had started so frighteningly with the scare of the cat fight seemed to lie sweet with happiness all around her. A cat—a kitten! Her very own.

How could it be? Millicent looked toward the closed door in happy bewilderment as if to ask, how had it come about that she could have a cat? Who'd known there was a kind of cat that wouldn't set off Mother's allergy? She looked down at Blue Angel. He *was* different.

Until now she'd never thought of different kinds of cats; she'd picked up kittens to feed and to play with and all that mattered was that they needed her. Blue Angel didn't need her. She needed him. But she had him, she proudly told herself.

It was so early it would be hours before she could ask Mother about her cat. Still, Mother was a light sleeper, maybe she was lying awake right now. Couldn't she take Blue Angel and see? Imagine cuddling up close to Mother with a cat! She had a thousand questions to ask about Blue Angel. Who had known? Oh, Sally must have been the one who knew Blue Angel wouldn't bring on allergy. But all of them, Mother and Carl, Dave and Sally, all of them planning it!

But for all her longing to ask questions, Millicent knew she shouldn't waken Mother. She looked at Blue Angel. She shouldn't waken him either. He'd had a strange night in a strange house—he needed to sleep. But it was hard to lie still—it was impossible. She had to talk to someone.

She slid off the bed, tiptoed to the window, pushed the curtains aside, and stood looking out into the darkness to where a street light rayed between houses and dimly lit a backyard. The backyard was Sarah's.

"Sarah," she whispered. "There *are* blue cats, and I've got one! He's right here in my room with me. My family gave him to me. He's the biggest surprise I've ever had."

She had spoken under her breath to the distant, sleeping Sarah then, bemusedly, she drifted back to the bed, lay down, chin cupped between her hands, face right over Blue Angel, and looked and loved and dreamed.

How had the family managed to keep everything so secret? How had they kept the little cat quiet the whole night? Oh, Dave and Sally must have kept him at their house until after she'd gone to bed. She could just see Mother putting him in the Easter basket, all

excited because she could hold a cat in her arms. Then they must have fed Blue Angel the very last thing, so he'd sleep.

Millicent rolled over on the bed hugging herself. The wonder of it! The miracle! The words sang themselves: "Miracle on Easter Morning!"

And to think it had started with a cat fight. A fight so fierce the one cat had slammed the other against their house so hard it had sounded like a door slamming shut.

A door . . . a window? Something cold and black fell down over her and wound around her. All her happiness caved in. Words came stumbling out: "Nobody gave you Blue Angel. Blue Angel was slammed through the window, the window you left unlocked yesterday."

As if she had been looking for proof she saw a clot of dried blood inside the torn tip of Blue Angel's ear. Yes, he had been in that fight—but she had to know, she had to go down to the window. Through the crack in the door as she gentled it shut she watched, but the little cat slept on, undisturbed by her leaving.

Millicent slipped soundlessly down the stairs, then in spite of herself gasped out as she stepped barefooted on the slippery, rolling little pile of chewed up, nibbled olive pits. She listened, scared, but there wasn't a sound in the house. She desolately rubbed her foot dry on the carpet—and here she'd been so proud that like her, her kitten liked olives. Liked them! He was so starved he'd have eaten anything.

She ran to the basement and climbed up on the workbench. No, the window wasn't locked. And, like Sarah, she could easily hold it open with a finger. She ran her fingertips along the underside of the window frame. Damp hairs clung. They were blue-gray! There was no doubt at all. The young cat had been Blue Angel. It was his hair that had been scrubbed out of his skin by the window falling shut like a trap as he'd rolled through into the basement.

It came over Millicent now in woeful tides. Nobody had given Blue Angel to her. Royal though he looked, he was a lost kitten, like all the rest of the alley kittens—driven, chased, and beaten by the big, fierce fighter cats.

Right then she heard a high, wild, banshee wailing coming from upstairs. The wails rose higher and higher. It was—it could be nothing but Blue Angel.

She raced up the stairs, praying that if Mother or Carl heard, they'd think it was a cat fight outside. She pushed her bedroom door open and scooped Blue

Angel up in one scared, swift motion. Weak with fright she sank down on the edge of her bed with him in her arms. He stretched up and rubbed his head and his cold, moist nose against her cheek. He was purring in crazy, hoarse spurts, as if telling her how glad he was to have her back again.

"Blue Angel, Blue Angel," Millicent whispered in his ear. "I won't leave you again ever! You're mine and you're always going to be mine."

Still, for all her fierce promising the only thing she could think to do was to reach out and lock her door. To her amazement the house stayed silent. Nothing happened, nobody came. But what was the good of locking herself up? With Mother's allergy she couldn't keep Blue Angel. And with his big voice she couldn't hide him.

Then suddenly it came to her. It had been Blue Angel she'd heard yesterday when she stood on the basement stairs waiting for Sarah to go. It hadn't been Sarah imitating—it had been Blue Angel. He hadn't sounded like a cat then, either, he'd sounded like a baby—no, more like a baby goat! At this miserable, unfortunate small joke, Millicent started crying. Blue Angel put a questioning paw on her quivering cheek. She hugged him and stopped her crying. She had things to do. With the little cat in her arms she got up and unlocked the door. He'd only be quiet if he was with her, and she must pick up the olive mess he'd made in the living room.

When she'd thought Blue Angel was an Easter present she'd figured they'd kept him quiet all night by feeding him. Well, she'd really feed him now. With Blue Angel in her arms she stole down the stairs.

Now, that must be the last bitten, chewed-off olive stone. Millicent dropped it in the bedraggled Easter basket and looked around. There, half pushed under a chair—Blue Angel must have played with it—she saw the toy cat they'd got for her again this Easter. If she needed any more proof here it was. Lucky she'd seen it. She picked it up and plunked it on her arm with Blue Angel. She looked around once more but it seemed there'd been no chocolate rabbit this year. Unless the little cat had eaten it! He was so starved, she could believe even that of him. Now she'd really feed him.

She eased the kitchen door open, grabbed a big dollop of hamburger out of the refrigerator and plopped it on top of the olive pits in the basket. Then with the little cat tight in her arm, the toy cat half pushed under him, she walked up the stairs. But half-way up, in a wild scramble and a fierce lunge, Blue Angel leaped from her arm to the basket, steadied himself with all four paws on its rim, and rode up, gobbling the meat.

The Easter basket with its strange load of olive pits, hamburger, and gorging kitten rubbed hard against Millicent's leg as she slid into her room.

chapter five

The Rats at the Trough

With her back against the bedroom door Millicent stood waiting. She had to wait until the big meal of hamburger took effect and Blue Angel went to sleep. If he began wailing again . . . .

"Please, please, let me think of a plan," she begged. She couldn't keep a cat in the same house with Mother, so she'd better start right now thinking of a place for Blue Angel. But where? What about under the porch? It was separated from the house by the foundation wall—could she keep Blue Angel there?

Not with Blue Angel's voice! He'd yell and yell, and he'd never let up unless she was down there with him. Once Mother and Carl were up they'd hear him the first thing.

On the bed Blue Angel hiccuped but instead of waking, sank deeper into sleep. Millicent looked at him in mothering fondness. He'd been so starved, he'd eaten all the hamburger even after all those olives. Now he was such a full little cat, he'd likely sleep and sleep and never wake enough to start yowling. Maybe if she covered him he'd sleep even sounder.

She went to the bed and placed her pillows on either side of him, and softly drew the covers over them. Then she went to her door and locked it.

Safe now, she lifted a tip of the covers and peered down the tunnel of pillows. Blue Angel opened an eye, looked at her annoyed, put a slow paw over his face, and went back to sleep.

Millicent gently replaced the covers.

But what was there to do? Where could she go with Blue Angel? She thought of the trap door to the attic in the ceiling of her closet. Could she put him up there? No, he'd start wailing right over Mother's and Carl's bedrooms. She opened her closet and stared up at the small trap door. There was so little time now—she must find a way that would work.

As if in solemn warning the clock downstairs struck six. A whole hour gone, and nothing planned that would work. If she was going to keep Blue Angel —and she was—she had to find a hideout, and the hideout had to be away from the house. She knew of only one place like that—the warehouse in the alley. It had been closed and locked for years, but there was one small hole in the back wall. Only she and the neighborhood cats knew of that way into the gloomy old building. Could she keep Blue Angel there?

She'd promised Mother long ago—oh, it must be two years ago—that she'd never even go near it again. Never as long as she lived! "Cross my heart and hope to die, Mama."

Millicent went to the window and opened the curtains. It was still gray outside, but she could see the sharp roof of the old warehouse rising above the other buildings in the rain-darkened morning. She stood there remembering her mother's scared words when she had caught her back of the old building. "Promise me, Mimi! You must promise me! You don't understand, but it's dangerous for little girls to go into empty buildings. Tramps and bums, all kinds of bad men come to places like this to hide and to

sleep. You could be killed! Millicent, I know you need to have a kitten but don't keep one in an awful place like this, even if you can't have one at home—it's too dangerous. I wish it could be different, but there's my allergy and I can't help it." She had been scared enough by her mother's words to promise anything. She had never gone into the warehouse again.

"Some day," Mother had kept promising, "some day my allergy will go away." But that day had never come, and so she'd settled for just secretly feeding and playing with kittens outside in the alley.

But now! It was so desperate now—what if she'd take Blue Angel and go back to the warehouse? Since she'd never gone back Mother most likely wouldn't remember or even think of the warehouse. If she kept Blue Angel there, he'd be close enough to feed, and every day she could play with him. Every night she'd lock him up in one of the small rooms in the warehouse loft.

Now, staring at the warehouse roof, she could see the whole empty place in her mind. The crawl hole must still be in the back wall, it had been so hidden by weeds and a small oil drum, wedged between the wall and a stumpy, misgrown tree.

She'd found the hole in the wall by following an

all-white cat. The cat had gone behind the thick weeds up against the warehouse wall, then just as she'd reached out her hands to grab him, the cat had disappeared into the building.

The cat—the first all-white cat she'd ever seen—had been so beautiful, she hadn't been able to stand losing him. Small as she'd been, she'd wrestled the oil drum from behind the wedging tree and had crawled in after the cat. There she'd been, inside the great hushed, dim room that was the empty warehouse. There hadn't been a sound, and behind the high, narrow, grimed, cobwebby windows had lain a quiet light like in a church.

The white cat had sat in the middle of the empty, dusty floor—there he'd sat, head turned, looking at her as she crawled in. Then he'd heard rats! He'd dashed up a rickety stairway to a loft on one side of the enormous room. He'd disappeared in one of the rooms up there. Then had come the terrified scuttling of so many rat feet that in the hollow, echoing building rat feet had sounded like thunder. But into the frantic scuttling had come a frightening silence, and out of that silence one piercing squeal.

She had stood terrified for one lone cat among the thundering army of rats. She'd raced up the rickety stairs to rescue the cat. But she'd come to a place where too many treads were missing, and she'd had to stop.

As she'd stood there clinging to the unsteady rail, the cat had silently appeared at the top of the stairs, his white head held high and reared back. For a moment she and the cat had stood staring at each other before in her horror she'd managed to turn and rush headlong down the shaky stairs. Behind her the cat had leaped the gap in the stairway, but in the jarring jump he'd dropped the rat, and the sound of the fall had thudded through the empty room.

Almost headless with horror, she'd fled from the cat, too blind with fear to find the crawl hole in the wall. But the cat, proud of his trophy, had wanted to bring her the rat. The cat had picked it up, and with it dangle-dragging between his front legs, he'd come on. In terror she'd run back and forth along the back wall of the horrible room, as if she herself were a trapped rat.

Suddenly the crawl hole had opened up to her eyes. Headlong she'd dived through it. But outside, she'd twisted around and there had been the cat with the rat. In the strength of her terror, she'd lifted the empty oil drum and slammed it tight between the wall and the stunted tree, so the cat couldn't possibly get out. She'd run home crying.

Before she'd got home she'd known she'd have to go back. The hole in the wall was the only opening, and if the cat couldn't get out, it would die of thirst. She'd pictured the whole army of starved rats, unable to get out of the warehouse for food, turning on the lone, locked-in cat.

Back at the warehouse as she'd lain on her knees wrestling the oil drum away from the hole, she'd caught a brief glimpse of the white cat. He'd sat washing himself in a spot of sunshine fallen through a broken window pane, high up in the wall.

But then she'd heard a stifled gasp behind her. There her mother had stood. And right there Mother had made her promise never to go near the warehouse again. Over and over she'd promised before Mother was satisfied. She'd never gone back.

Now she was going to break her promise. She had to. There was no other place, no other way. Stiff-legged with determination, she walked from the window, unlocked and opened the door, and listened for sounds in the house.

It had to be now. She turned, pulled back the covers, and picked up Blue Angel. Sudden light made her turn to the window. It was light! It couldn't be, so suddenly—but it was. The sun had broken through the clouds. The first glint of sunlight glanced off the steep slant of the warehouse roof. At one end of the high roof a sagging length of eavestrough gleamed. The trough had trapped rain water that had run off the roof, and sunlight shone in the water. Now as the sun glinted over the slant of the gray slate roof there came thick, gray, scuttling shadows—a whole army of scurrying rats. Sunlight kept streaming, and the rats kept coming as if racing the sun. Snapping, quarreling, biting, they fought for position at the sagged, flooded eavestrough. Then as the sun rose and sharpened, the rats went quiet, and all their sharp faces in one long row dipped down to the water as they drank.

Suddenly the sun cleared the distant roof, hit Millicent's window, and shone blindingly in her eyes. Sunlight woke Blue Angel. Purring, he stretched up to Millicent's face. When she could see again, the long row of rats was gone, as if gone up and melted into the morning sun. They were gone from the roof as if they'd never been; they were back in the warehouse.

And Millicent knew that whatever happened now,

she couldn't take Blue Angel to the warehouse among the rats. How could she take her sweet, young, trusting kitten, kissing and butting her chin, into a place like that?

Then it was too late. Suddenly down the hall there was the sound of water running. Her mother was up. Whatever would come now, it was too late for the warehouse. In her relief, Millicent crooned over the kitten in her arms. Blue Angel made tiny moans of fondness, chewed gently on her thumb, then nestled down against her and faded into sleep.

chapter six

Ladder of Shelves

After the first moment of panic on hearing the shower, it was as if Millicent's mind was made up for her by the sound of the water, as if she'd known all along what she'd do when this moment came. There was nothing now but the secret room under the porch.

She ran with the sleeping cat to her locked bedroom door, stood listening for any change of sound. In the near bathroom Mother was still showering. Now was the time for the quick dash downstairs.

Millicent shifted Blue Angel to one arm, but as she reached for the key in the lock, before her startled eyes the knob of her door began turning. In the sound of water running, she hadn't heard anyone coming down the hall. The knob stopped. "Hey?" Carl's voice demanded. "Mimi, Millidollar, you still asleep? . . . Hey, her door's locked," Carl muttered to himself. Loudly he demanded, "Mimi, you all right? Why's your door locked?"

On her side of the door, clutching Blue Angel, hand over his face to smother any sound, Millicent kept deathly still.

"Mimi, open this door!" Carl yelled out.

Down the hall the water shut off in the shower, and Mother called, "Carl, what is it? What's wrong?"

Millicent was caught, nailed to her room, and there was no escape possible. There was only one thing left she could do—get the kitten into the attic. She noiselessly opened her closet, looked up at the ceiling. There was the trap door, but how to reach it? There was nothing tall enough in her room she could stand on to open it and shove Blue Angel through into the attic.

At one end of the closet was a tier of shelves. Could she use the shelves as a ladder? There was no time to think whether she could or couldn't. She tossed Blue Angel over her shoulder and reached for the bottom shelf. The little cat shifted and crawled around just enough to fit himself around her neck. There he clung, nails digging in, but Millicent didn't feel it as she climbed. Supporting herself with one hand on top of the narrow ledge of the frame of the closet door, she could lean back far enough to touch the trap door in the ceiling, but had to lunge up to shove it out of its frame. She lunged, the trap door flew open, but the shelf under her tipped. Everything around her feet slid from the shelf to the closet floor. Millicent clawed and grabbed to catch herself by the frame of the trap door in the ceiling. She dangled, feet swinging. The terrified cat leaped from her shoulder. up through the trap door opening, and scooted away into the attic.

Down in the room the door rattled, and Mother called out, "Mimi, are you all right? Why is your door locked? Millicent!"

In that unnerving moment Millicent let go her hold, but landed on blankets that had spilled to the floor, so she didn't make too much of a thud. Picking herself up, she eyed the trap door, but there was no way to close it. She hastily pushed the closet shut, ran to unlock her bedroom door.

"Millicent, do you hear me?" Mother sounded

frantic. "Carl, bring a key," she called down the hall. "All these old locks are the same."

"I'm coming, I'm here at the door," Millicent cried out angrily. "Give me a chance, can't you? The key is stuck." She made it grate in the lock. "Blue Angel, be quiet," she whisper-begged toward the ceiling, then opened the door to face her mother, as Carl came up, a key ready in his hand.

Mother started to come into the room, but suddenly put her hand to her throat, and whispered out, "There is a cat here! Can you take care of it, Carl? I'll have to run and take my allergy medicine. If I can catch it right away . . . . " In the hall she turned. "Mimi, how could you? Easter, and Sally and your brother coming . . . ." Hands over her mouth and nose, she hurried away toward her room. Carl stood looking after her, then in a loud voice that he must have wanted Mother to hear, he ordered, "Okay, hand me that cat."

Millicent swept her hands wide to show there was no cat in the room.

Down the hall Mother's door slammed shut. Carl winked, and his tone changed and became friendly. Softly he said, "Okay, Millidollar. But little did I think you'd make me get rid of a cat on Easter morning—and even before breakfast! Three days in the stocks for you, you miserable cat lover."

Millicent suddenly had hope. Carl was all different now Mother wasn't here. He'd even winked. She gave him a deep, pleading look, then couldn't help herself and looked toward the closet.

"Oh, so that's where you've got the cat. Getting tricky, ain't you?" Carl swept his hands, imitating her. "Sure, he's not here in your room—he's up in the attic." He jerked the closet door open, immediately saw the open trap door in the ceiling. "So you climbed the shelves. Well, I'm too heavy for that, so you get up there and drop the cat down to me. You must have known you couldn't keep a cat there!"

"Carl!" Millicent grabbed his arm. "Oh, Carl, he isn't a stray. He's blue—cream and blue—and he's even got blue eyes! And I didn't bring him in, he came. He was in the living room. He'd found the Easter basket, and—imagine—he likes olives! He ate all your olives!" In her earnestness to show Carl the wonder and strangeness of the little cat, she pulled the basket from under the bed and showed him the bedraggled, ratty mess of olive pits.

Carl stared at the basket. "Now come off it, Sis. How could a cat get in the house? And olives!"

"Through the basement window," Millicent told Carl honestly. "Yesterday Sarah came to borrow my jump rope. It was in the basement, so I threw it out to her, and I . . . I, I guess I forgot to lock the window."

"Wow!" Carl exclaimed. "You're getting better and better. Well, if you're going to lie, make it a big one, I always say." He looked almost pleased with her. "But what a whopper! Guess instead of Milli-dollar, I'll start calling you Trixie, you're getting so tricky."

"But it's true!"

"Sure, sure," Carl agreed. "Now you just get yourself up there and get that blue cat. A blue cat full of green olives, now I've heard it all."

Millicent stared at Carl in utter unbelief. Tricky! He'd *tricked* her by winking and acting friendly, as if he were on her side. And she'd been silly enough to think that if Carl saw the beautiful little cat, he'd be willing to help her.

She didn't move, wouldn't take a step toward the closet. Her mouth tight, she stood and looked at Carl as if wondering how she could ever have believed in him.

Carl saw it. "Get it through your stubborn head," he said sourly, "it won't do you any good to turn mulish. All I have to do is get the stepladder and get him myself."

Millicent didn't move. Hopeless as it was, she had to fight to the last. Blue Angel was hers!

Then from her room Mother called out, "Mimi, do you know where that new box of allergy pills is?"

Carl looked at Millicent, but she drew up her shoulders and shrugged.

"I'm coming, I'll find it," Carl called to Mother. He started from the room.

"Carl!" Millicent blurted in a last desperate try. "Carl, Blue Angel's so beautiful, he—he's royal! And if you just throw him out, he'll starve—he'll die in that alley."

"Royal, huh?" Carl said. "And you've already given him a name." He brushed her aside. "We'll let him be royal out in the country."

He must have known he'd said too much. At the door he turned. "Look, Sis, stop worrying. I won't just toss him out of the car. I'll let him out near a farm somewhere in the country. Farmers have lots of milk for cats, and their barns are always full of mice." Carl grinned suddenly. "But a blue cat won't even have to catch them. When they see a blue cat, they'll drop dead for him."

It was meant to be funny, it was only cruel. Millicent blazed with resentment. She couldn't speak.

"Now get that cat down, while I help Mother," Carl said from the hall. "You'll see, some day Mom's allergy will just go away, and then you can have the house full of cats—even the attic."

Some day! All of them—always they trotted out that old promise of some day. Some day wouldn't help Blue Angel.

Down the hall Carl opened Mother's door, and even that far away Millicent could hear her gasping. Still rebellious, Millicent felt guilty at the same time. Then the thought hit. Could she get the kitten down and still have time to put him under the porch while they were hunting for the medicine?

She ran to the closet as the front doorbell rang.

"Answer it, will you, Mimi? That's likely Dave and Sally," Carl yelled from Mother's room.

Millicent did not answer, did not move.

"Oh, she must be up in the attic. I told her to get that cat down," Carl called back to Mother as he himself went down to answer the door.

Softly Millicent started to close her bedroom door, but below she heard Carl open the front door, and say, "Hi, Dave. Hi, Sally. I suppose you came to take Mother to the Sunrise Service? I was going to go too, but your little sister took care of that. Mom's sick with her allergy. Mimi brought a cat in the house—she's got him up in the attic. Gosh, I've got to run, we can't find Mom's allergy pills."

"Mimi and cats!" Dave started to laugh, then stopped himself. "You mean to say she actually brought one in the house in spite of Mother's allergy?"

"Yeah," Carl said sourly. "The darned kid knows better too. Lied like a trooper. Claims this cat got in by a basement window she left unlocked, and that he's blue—even his eyes. *Royal*, she says . . . . Hey, Dave, why don't we just jump in your car? I've got to try and find a drugstore open and get Mother a new box of pills. Sally, will you run up to Mother?"

"All right," Millicent heard Sally say. "But you know, Carl, there are blue cats. It must be a blue-point Siamese. They do have blue eyes, and they *are* royal."

Carl grunted. Down below Dave's car started up, and almost the next moment Sally knocked at Millicent's door. "Mimi? I'll be with you as soon as I've looked at Mom."

At Sally's hurried, kind words Millicent dissolved. But at that moment there was a hard thump in the closet. The thump was followed by an outraged yowl. Blue Angel must have jumped all the way from the attic to the floor. Now he yowled and kept yowling, demanding attention.

Sally came running back down the hall, burst into the room, and ran to the closet. "Oh, the darling," she said, and started to pick Blue Angel up. "I had one as a child." But then she stepped back. "I've got to tend to your mother first, but then I'll be back, and we'll work something out." She put a hasty arm around Millicent, then ran.

Hope had streamed into the room, the way morning sunshine streams through a window. But with Sally went the hope, and Blue Angel stood wailing. Millicent scooped up the cat and squeezed her cupped hand over his face to silence him. With his voice, what was the use? And what could Sally do? In moments Carl and Dave would be back, and they'd take Blue Angel away. What could Sally do against them? Sally didn't know how awful Mother's allergy could be. Just wait till Sally saw what it did to Mother.

But with Carl and Dave gone wasn't this her last and only chance? Millicent did not waver a moment. The little cat tight in her arms, she flew down the stairs to the kitchen, unlocked the back door, and ran over the porch to the phonograph. With her one free hand she pried and pulled at the false bottom until it came up with all its belongings still on it, and dropped Blue Angel into the darkness under the porch.

As she'd expected Blue Angel began yowling as soon as he hit the ground. Millicent dropped the false bottom and raced to pull the back door shut, so they wouldn't hear him up in the house. She stopped. What was the use? With his voice they'd know in a minute that he was under the porch.

Let the back door stand open, let them think she'd run out into the alley with Blue Angel. Let them think she'd run away from home!

Once more Millicent opened the secret bottom of the phonograph without removing the garden stuff that rested on it, but this time wide enough for herself. Garden tools danced and banged, and the thin rattle of spilling fertilizer was in her ears as she slid feet first through the partially opened phonograph bottom. She dropped down into the darkness. Above her the false bottom fell shut with a hard, tinny rattle of tools.

Under the porch Millicent poked about for the flashlight. Her fingers sank down into loose, dry dirt, but she couldn't, wouldn't let herself think a single scared thought in the crawly darkness. Then Blue Angel rubbed himself against her knee. She stooped down to the sound of his purr. Blue Angel was standing up on his hind legs to reach her face. With cold nose and cool lips he kiss-brushed her chin. Blue Angel was thanking her.

chapter seven

Fugitive

There was a scrape of tires, then Millicent heard the sounds of car doors slamming shut, and Carl's and Dave's voices as they hurried into the house by way of the basement door in the driveway. Under the porch Millicent puzzled why she could hear her brothers even inside the house. Oh, she'd not only left the back door to the porch wide open, in her hurry she must have left the kitchen door to the living room open too. Plainly she heard Carl say, "Dave, look! The back door's wide open. Look, you run up and give Sally the new medicine, and check Mimi's room, because if she's not there or in the attic, she's run out with that cat!"

Carl came out on the porch. He began softly calling her name, more saying it than calling it, as if he knew she was near and he expected her to answer. But Carl's voice was too soft and too friendly. Millicent kept her hand tight over Blue Angel's face.

Now Dave stepped onto the porch. "Stop that calling. Mother might hear!" Dave closed the door.

Carl immediately stopped calling, but then it was worse—he began pacing, and Dave started pacing with him. The pounding of their feet made a roar under the hollow porch. Through the thunder of feet Millicent heard Carl say, "She can't be far—there wasn't time— so the alley's the most likely place. She always goes there to play with cats."

"Hey, sure—that warehouse down the alley!" Dave exclaimed. "Remember? She tried to keep a cat there once."

Millicent heard it in dismayed surprise. Her brothers knew about the warehouse and the white cat— Mother had told them. Did they know about the false bottom in the phonograph? She crouched low, expecting their feet to stop at the phonograph and to hear its door squeak open, and she right under it! Clutching Blue Angel, Millicent crawled toward the partition. As she crawled her brothers paced above her, and gritty dust, loosened by their pounding feet, shook down on her bent neck as she fought the struggling little cat, terrified at the roar all around him.

Blue Angel twisted and snaked, in wild fright he bit her hand and clawed out of her grasp. Millicent lunged to grab him, but bumped her head against the unseen partition so hard, she had to kneel face down with her hands held over her head to keep from crying out. The little cat was gone in the dark. He must have scooted through the crawl hole into whatever was beyond the partition. She couldn't move to go after him. The nausea of pain came over her in waves, the thunder of her brothers' footsteps pounded into the pain. At last her brothers clumped down the porch steps, and on into the yard.

It sounded as if Carl had gone into the garage. Millicent heard him talking to her as if she were right there in the garage. He opened the car doors, he even opened the trunk of his car.

"Not here," he called out. Then all sound of her brothers was gone.

Beyond the partition Blue Angel did not make the slightest sound. Alone in the black outer room Millicent gratefully remembered that the spray gun was somewhere near—the flashlight too. The flashlight had gone out yesterday when she'd dropped it, but if the bulb hadn't broken, wouldn't light be wonderful? She crawled back to the phonograph. To keep her mind off the gritty dry dust squeezing up in little spurts between her fingers, Millicent thought hard about the warehouse. If she'd gone there, Dave and Carl would be finding her right now and taking Blue Angel away. Mother had told them about the warehouse, but it couldn't be that anybody knew about the false bottom, else Dave and Carl would have come straight to the phonograph. She was safe—for a while.

But she mustn't only get out of this room, the blanket and all her belongings had to come out too. If they did know, or if they remembered, they'd come and shine a light. Nothing in the room must look different, everything had to be as it always was, everything had to go behind the partition.

Then her hand came down on the flashlight. Her eyes actually teared in her relief—at last light. But when she pushed the switch, nothing happened. She clicked and clicked the useless flashlight, but it stayed dead. In sudden despairing fury she flung it away. It crashed in the dark against the partition. It sounded as if it had shattered.

Light or no light, she must still get all her stuff behind the partition—the smashed flashlight too. She wouldn't think about great hairy spiders stilting along on their thin legs, nor about scuttling bugs that stupidly came right at you and up you—just set her teeth and crawl ahead.

In the dark her hand came down on the round cannister of the spray gun. The spray gun! But that's what she'd do! Spray ahead of her wherever she crawled, spray everything dead! Then she'd feel safe! Spray gun in hand, she crawled along, pumping and pumping the handle with all her might. Then in the far room she heard Blue Angel sneeze, sneeze, and sneeze. She dropped the gun to whisper to him, but began sneezing herself. In her terror of spiders and beetles and all running things she'd gone at her spraying too fiercely for this tight, closed space.

Through her sneezes she heard the little cat come sneezing toward her. Then, "Nnn-iauw!" he said in indignant protest right under her face. He began rubbing against her, trying to purr through his sneezes. In between purrs he indignantly questioned her over and over in his funny, harsh voice. She gathered him in, gratefully told him she loved him, but that she had to go back and get her blanket and things. He answered in his strange uncatlike voice—he couldn't even say "Miauw"—he made it an "N." But he wanted to be near her, and in the blackness he made himself her guide. He could see, and she could follow his purrs. With the tiger and teddy bear, flashlight and spray gun rolled in her blanket, Millicent followed him right through the low, rounded crawl space. His upright, straight, happy tail fanned her face.

But when inside the partition Millicent dropped her belongings, he jumped away. At least now she was safe, even if they shone a light down through the phonograph. And once through the crawl hole Millicent found that this room was lighter. The porch steps were above this inner room; outside light filtered through the cracks under the steps.

The cracks under each step were wide. Millicent was almost sure that if she could dare to push her face among the stringy, dirty cobwebs hanging thick from every step, she could see the backyard and watch for her brothers to come back. She didn't dare use any more spray. Could she use the long, limp

tiger as a duster to knock the cobwebs down? No—
the teddy bear, he was stiffer, he was sturdy. Grab
him by the feet, hold him like a long-handled duster,
and whack the dirty cobwebs down.

Where was Blue Angel? Her eyes were getting used
to the filtered, dim light, and Millicent caught a
small movement. There in the farthest corner, on a
small mound of dirt up against the cement wall of the
house sat Blue Angel, gravely washing from his nose
and whiskers the dust that clung after all his sneezes.
There he sat unafraid, like a little king on his throne.

It was calming. How clever he was, that was the
very place for their bed! The raised dirt end would
make a sort of pillow. She'd pull the beach blanket
over it and place the tiger on top. With his limp body
draped over the mound, long legs and tail hanging
down, he would make a fine pillow, and her hair
wouldn't be in the dirt. She was calm now like Blue
Angel, and calm, she felt thankful for the blanket to
spread over the dirt, thankful for the tiger pillow.
The pencil-thin lines of light under the steps would
let her see enough to find Blue Angel quickly when
her brothers came. If their voices suddenly spoke,
Blue Angel might answer. He was the talkingest cat
she had ever known. He talked back! He tried to keep

up a conversation like a person. It was going to be dangerous.

Where was he now? In just the time she had made their bed, he was gone again through the crawl hole, back into the outer room. Millicent couldn't face crawling back into that total dark. "Blue Angel, come here!" she nervously snapped out, and sat alarmed, hand clapped over her own mouth, but, remembering the dirt her hands had crawled in, she spat.

Then there wasn't a sound anywhere, and Blue Angel didn't come. Where was he? Why was he so still? Suddenly just sitting there, not knowing what was happening anywhere, was more than Millicent could stand. She grabbed the teddy bear and crawled over to the steps. With eyes shut she swung the fuzzy bear back and forth among the stringy, sticky webs filled with the wings of flies and the dead, sucked-out shells of beetles and bugs.

At last when Millicent opened her eyes the light was coming much clearer through the cracks. The cobwebs were mostly down, stickily wrapped around the head of the teddy bear she flung far from her. He'd landed, shoe button eyes down, under the bottom step, rump, thick with cobwebs, sticking up. It

was so silly, Millicent laughed, and then she dared put her hands down in the dirt and push her head under the steps to peer out through the cracks. There was nothing and nobody in the yard. But she'd put her hand down on something hard that looked like a barrel top, half buried. Then she knew it wasn't a barrel top—it was the half-moon door that belonged in the crawl hole. Excitedly she tugged it free. Now she'd be able to keep Blue Angel right in the room with her.

The scraping noise as she dragged out the little half-door brought Blue Angel rushing. He pounced on it as it came free, and as Millicent started sliding it toward the crawl hole, he leaped on it and proudly rode it.

Millicent fitted the door into the crawl hole. It fit so tight, she had to push so hard, the fine dirt of the floor squeezed and gritted between her toes. Her toes! She hadn't even thought of slippers, hadn't even noticed until now. With Blue Angel she fled on hands and knees to the beach blanket. Safely in the middle of the big blanket, Millicent stroked and stroked the cat as she squirmily tried to rub her feet clean.

Above them the back door opened. Millicent cupped her hand over Blue Angel's mouth. Strangely, no footsteps came on the porch. It must be that whoever had opened the door was just standing there, listening. There was no sound of harsh breathing, so it couldn't be Mother. Sally? It must be Sally. Blue Angel was beginning to struggle—he liked Sally. Millicent rubbed her face against his to distract his attention. He roughly licked her face, and purred for Sally.

But instead of Sally, Carl spoke. Millicent hadn't heard him come through the back yard. "Gosh, Sally, am I glad you're down here," Carl was saying. "Any sign of Mimi? I came back to get my car, but didn't want to go in the house so Mother'd know."

"Not a sign," Sally answered. "But your mom's fine—she's resting. I've been rummaging in Mimi's room, hoping to find some clue. And, of course, you've had no luck or you wouldn't be here for the car."

"No." Carl sounded worried. "Dave's still looking through all the likely hidy-holes along the alley, but she wasn't anywhere we looked. We even broke into that warehouse where she tried to keep a cat, but she hadn't been there—not a mark in the dust."

"What about that dreary little girl I've heard her talk about?" Sally suddenly asked.

"Sarah?" Carl couldn't help chuckling. "Oh, we went there. Nobody up—all still asleep."

"Was Sarah?" Sally demanded. "Suppose she tossed pebbles up at Sarah's window, and Sarah let her in."

"Not Sarah!" Carl sounded sure. "She's scared of everything, and that includes cats. That's why the two of them don't get along better."

Under the porch Millicent grinned. Carl knew Sarah!

"Well, must get going. I'm doing the farther alleys with the car—it's quicker."

"Yes, but what good is it? Carl! I'm worried. None of Millie's clothes are missing—even her slippers are under the bed. No little girl would go far, barefoot in pajamas."

"Gosh, no, I guess not," Carl said slowly. "Except, you don't know Millicent and cats. She'd do anything to hang on to a cat—I guess almost go naked."

Under the porch Millicent grinned again. Carl knew her too!

"Well, I can search the house again," Sally said. "But I don't think they're anywhere in the house. Siamese are such talkers, she'd never keep him quiet.

But, Carl, there's a detective lives next door to my folks—let me call him for advice."

"No!" Carl said. "At least, not yet. And don't say anything like that to Mother. It'll take about five-ten minutes to cruise through the neighborhood, by that time Dave should be back too. Then we'll see."

The car started up and backed down the drive. Sally crossed over the porch and went into the house. The back door closed behind her. Millicent stared up at the porch floor in horror. The police! The police coming to hunt her! She held Blue Angel close, weakly laid her head on the tiger. Now if she didn't come out, they'd call the police. The police would come and find her. Fugitive from justice—the old phrase from some story crazily popped into her mind. She was a fugitive!

It was petrifying scary. She hugged Blue Angel to her so hard, he hissed out at her and bit her arm.

chapter eight

The Big Policeman

Out of the Sunday morning silence a drift sound of bells from far across the town stole under the porch and spun soft Easter music around Millicent. She cried a little for the lonely loveliness of the bells, and lay forlorn and frightened. The bells sang peace and happiness, but inside the house Sally was calling the police.

Millicent was scared enough, she caught herself wishing that she had gone with Blue Angel to the warehouse after all. By now they'd have been caught; it would all have been over.

It was a mean, weak thought, for it would all have been over for Blue Angel too—he'd have been taken away. She shook off the treacherous thought, but in its place a new thought came. It was sure now that nobody knew of this place under the porch. Then if Sally hadn't called the police, nobody would come. Only night would come, and in the black night she'd still be under the porch with the things that come out in the dark.

Thankfully, Millicent reminded herself that long before night Blue Angel would be yowling with hunger. They'd hear him, and she'd have to give him up. Somehow that would be different—she wouldn't have given him up, he would have given himself away. The thought was so tempting, she woke the little cat by falsely whispering to him, "You have to stay quiet whatever happens."

She needed him to talk to, but Blue Angel struggled away from her as if he knew her Judas thoughts. In some cowardly, secret pocket of her, Millicent actually found herself hoping that away from her, Blue Angel would begin his terrible yelling. But across the room she heard him industriously sharpen his nails in wood, then become quiet.

Millicent lay feeling miserable and ashamed, and so false, it was almost a hollow feeling. Hollow! She was hungry—that's why she felt hollow. She'd fed

Blue Angel but she'd had nothing to eat the whole long morning, and she'd been up for hours. As she thought about it, her hunger became an actual pain. She put both hands over her stomach. What if she got appendicitis down here? She imagined having to be found in the dark, then hoisted up through the phonograph. No, they'd have to tear up the porch floor. Men in white would come crawling under the porch with a stretcher, and an ambulance would be waiting tight up against the porch steps to rush her to the hospital.

It was silly and far-fetched, but still she was hungry enough that the next moment she was imagining herself and Blue Angel creeping up from under the porch in the dead of night, and slipping into the house to steal food and milk. She couldn't! All the doors would be locked.

The sobering fact ended her dramatic imaginings. Then a new drift of bells, so far away their sound was just a hum under the tight porch, made Millicent lie back and close her eyes. "Oh, it's quiet," she whispered to herself. Then she slept.

Millicent dozed, woke, dozed again. The next thing

she knew, Blue Angel landed hard on her stomach. As she scared fully awake, she heard the back door opening, and heavy feet came on the porch. As if to get away from the thunderous sound Blue Angel pushed his head under Millicent's arm. She cradled him, hand hard over his mouth. Her brothers were back! Right above her a strange voice asked, "You found absolutely nothing?"

"Nothing," Carl's voice answered. "Between Dave and me we didn't miss a street or alley as far as she possibly could have run—and a darn sight farther."

"Now what do we do?" Dave asked, his voice scared and worried.

Under the porch Millicent shook herself. She'd actually fallen asleep! Maybe she'd just nodded, she didn't know, maybe she'd slept hours. There were no Easter bells now. Above her the men stopped still as the back door opened.

"Oh, I thought I'd heard voices," Millicent heard Sally say. Sally sounded surprised. "Carl, I didn't ask Detective Waters to come—I called to ask his advice. But the police don't fool around when it comes to little girls that have disappeared. He just took over." Sally sounded apologetic and uneasy and guilty.

"It's all right," Carl assured her. "Detective Waters

drove up just as Dave and I came back in the car. We've been talking."

"Close the door," Dave ordered Sally. "If you heard us, Mother can. But what do we do now?" he asked the detective again. "As Carl told you, we covered the whole neighborhood and went a lot farther than she could have run."

"I'm afraid that's exactly it," the detective said. "You went too far. Sally told me on the phone that your sister'd left barefoot in pajamas, so it follows she's holed up some place close. Some simple, obvious place none of us has thought of."

"For example," Carl demanded.

"For example, in some garage or under some neighbor's porch, or in a covered trash box. Could even be an empty trash can, pulling the cover over her and the cat."

"Nonsense," Dave snorted. "She's a little girl."

"Sure," the detective said, "and I'm the father of five little girls. I know only one thing about little girls —they're likely to do absolutely anything."

Somebody made a noise.

"All right," the detective said. "Your sister now, the way she dotes on cats—don't you think she'd do almost anything for a special, blue-eyed kitten, when all her life she's been denied any kind of a cat? Anyway, shall we try it? Sally, maybe you'd better go with them. With you along, the neighbors won't get so disturbed as when they see a couple of men poking around in their yards. I can appreciate you don't want the neighbors to know yet. But go in their yards and poke under their porches and into everything, even if it makes you feel like fools. If people come out tell them you're looking for a lost puppy—a lost puppy excuses everything. And when no one's around keep softly calling to Millicent. After hiding this long, it may take very little to lure her out, especially with Sally along. But I'm thinking she isn't far from this house. In a way little girls are like cats, they're attached to home. Little boys run and run, then don't know what to do about it, except to run some more. Girls are smarter."

A sudden silence fell. The back door opened. It was Mother! "Thank goodness, you're here, Detective Waters," Mother said. "I'm feeling much better—I can't stay upstairs another minute. Now, what can I do?"

"Oh, that's good that you're feeling better," Dave said. "And don't worry, with Sergeant Waters directing, we'll soon have her back."

"Off you go," the detective ordered. He waited until obediently they had clumped down the steps, then said to Mother in an ordinary, calming voice, "I really sent them off to give them something to do and keep them from underfoot. But Mrs. Harding, you were a little girl once yourself. I want you to go through the whole house and look at everything through a little girl's eyes. Where would you hide?"

"I was a little girl in this very house," Mother said hopefully. "I'll look with her eyes and with mine—maybe I know a few hideouts she's never thought of." The hoarse throatiness was gone from Mother's voice. The back door closed after her.

After Mother left there was absolute quiet. The detective must have stood thinking, now he began to pace the length of the porch. The floor bent with the great weight of the man, even the joists under the floor bowed. Fine dirt loosened and sifted down like stiff, gritty rain. Millicent grabbed a loose end of the beach blanket and pulled it over herself and Blue Angel. He mustn't sneeze. She held her hand over the little cat's mouth. Scarily, thunderously the big detective marched back and forth. Under the porch everything rumbled.

Blue Angel struggled, terrified in the great noise

of the heavy footsteps. Then he sneezed, muffled in the palm of Millicent's hand he sneezed again. Millicent's heart stopped as above her the detective's feet stopped.

That moment Mother abruptly opened the back door. Her voice came in a rush. "Now I am scared! Her old teddy bear and a toy tiger are gone—a beach blanket too." Then Mother was crying. "She planned it, she intended to do it. She didn't just run out— she'd planned a hideout."

"Good," the policeman said. "Much better she planned it than if she just rushed off in her pajamas." He took big steps across the porch. "Come on, let's sit down on the steps here."

When Millicent dared to poke her head from under the blanket she could faintly see their movements through the narrow cracks under the steps.

Mother was crying. Millicent began crying with her. "Mother," she wanted to call out, "I'm right here." She swallowed the words.

Mother sniffed and sniffed. By the cracks Millicent could see the detective stretch his leg straight out to get at his handkerchief. Mother blew her nose and made muffled apologies. "I'm sorry. Oh, and here I sit leaning against you . . . it's a comfort though."

"That's why I was made so broad and ample," the detective joked. "And you notice I carry an ample handkerchief too."

"Thanks." Mother blew her nose once more. "I'll return it."

"One of my little girls hemstitched it for me—her first job as you no doubt can see. Wave it as a flag when your Millicent's back."

"Back! Ah, you are a comfort," Mother said softly. "But what do you make of her carrying things out of the house?"

"That she isn't far. She wouldn't have carried her things very far. Were you gone from the house yesterday?"

"In the afternoon for about two hours. What with Easter dinner I needed some last-minute things. But it was the only time I was gone."

"Well," the policeman said. "So now we know that if she planned it, she moved her things out of the house while you were gone. Had there been a cat in the house yesterday?"

"No," Mother said positively. "That's where my allergy makes me a good detective. I'm sure there was no cat until the one in the night that came up through the basement window she left unlocked."

"Let's try it for fit," the detective said. "Let's put it all together. She discovered her hideout yesterday afternoon, most likely quite by accident, because it seems to have nothing to do with the blue cat. The hideout came first. And it was all done in the two hours you were gone, but she told you that her friend Sarah had come along. So Sarah, no doubt, interrupted Millicent's plan. You talked to Sarah on the telephone. You feel sure Sarah isn't in on it?"

"Sarah knows nothing but the business of the jump rope," Mother said. "And I believe it, if for no other reason than that Sarah doesn't like cats. Sarah isn't adventurous like Millicent, and she's a great talker. Millicent wouldn't let her in on anything secret."

"So? Then your Mimi did it all alone, and most likely before she knew of the blue cat. We've got to assume that the cat actually came into the house of itself last night for why, when she had a hideout, would she bring the cat into the house? She knew your allergy would nose him out in a minute."

"Nose is the word," Mother said unhappily. She sniffed, sniffed again. "Is my allergy coming back?" she asked. "Or is it rose spray? Garden spray sometimes sets off my allergy too. I keep it in the bottom of that phonograph-planter there. The spray gun must be leaking."

"So that's what I've been smelling—I couldn't identify it," the big policeman said. But he did not move from the steps to go to the phonograph-planter to investigate. Millicent lay tight waiting for his footsteps. It was as if the man she had never seen in her life knew all she had done, and all she had planned. It was as if he knew exactly what had gone on in her mind. As if he'd watched her!

"Now then," Detective Waters spoke up, "it rained last night, and everything was sopping wet this morning, but she ran out just in pajamas and on bare feet to her hideout. You said none of her clothes and shoes were missing. And she hadn't put any in the hideout the day before. Where would a hideout like that have to be? Don't you see? *Right here in the house.*"

"It just can't be," Mother said. "I've been over everything twice—it's not in the house." Suddenly Mother sneezed. "Goodness," she said, "my allergy's back. I'll go and search the house again. I have to do something!"

The policeman had got up when Mother got up, but the back door closed, and he sat down again. He drummed his heels, and Millicent could see the flash of his polished shoes. Suddenly the flash and the drumming were gone. But the policeman hadn't gone. He'd turned, and now was kneeling on the bottom step, peering with one eye through the crack underneath the tread of the top step. Millicent could see the white of his one peering eye. She worriedly told herself he couldn't possibly see her in the dark.

"Well, Mimi," the detective said in a most ordinary voice, just as if he plainly saw her. "I could figure it out for myself, but why don't you just tell me how you and Blue Angel got under there? I could figure it out, but I want the two of us to have a chat before those big brothers, or even your mother, come back."

"How did you know?" Millicent choked out.

"I didn't. I'm good, but your mother's allergy really did the detecting. The cat got her even through the cracks under these steps. I suppose you go down through the phonograph-planter, don't you?"

"It's got a false bottom," Millicent told him readily, and strangely, almost felt sorry that the big man hadn't solved it. But he would have! Oh, he was smart.

The policeman's thundering, floor-bowing steps hurried over the porch. "I'll be right down—well, at

least my head will," he called through the phonograph. "I've got to see what it's like under there."

"You can't," Millicent warned, to stop him in time.
She started fast as she could for the crawl hole. "You
can't—you're way too big and heavy, the way you
sound."

The detective didn't hear her. He was rattling the
garden things out of the phonograph.

When Millicent pried and tugged the crawl hole
open, there he was in the outer room—at least his
head was. His big round face hung down through
the bottom of the phonograph, all puffed out, because
he had a flashlight in his mouth to keep his hands
free. There he hung but the flashlight shone on Millicent. She looked at him, and he at her, upside down.

Then he dropped the flashlight because he'd started
to say, "Hmn." The flashlight rolled, then shone
against the front wall of the porch. He said, "Hmn,"
again, clearer now without the flashlight. "So a partition down here to make two rooms. A secret entrance through a false bottom in a phonograph, a
crawl hole in a partition. Look! Even squares marked
out in the front wall the size of windows. Somebody
way back started something here he never finished—
my guess would be a secret clubhouse for boys. Boys

like to be secret. . . . Hey, where's that famous blue cat?"

"He got scared with you upside down. I couldn't hold him when he saw your face all puffed out with a flashlight sticking out of it—you did look like Halloween," Millicent told him.

The detective laughed. "You're not scared of me, and that's good. Golly, Millidollar—that's what Carl calls you, isn't it?—would you mind standing up in the cabinet to talk to me? I've got to pull out, all the blood's rushing down to my head, and I sort of need it for brains right now."

Millicent took time to pick up the flashlight and hand it to him, then she obeyed. It was good to stand up straight. Outside, sitting crosslegged on the porch floor, the detective looked at her by the daylight streaming into the phonograph cabinet, and she wasn't a bit scared of him. "Know why Carl calls me Millidollar?" she said in a delighted rush. "He says Millicent is only one thousandth of a cent and I am easily worth one thousandth of a dollar."

"I agree with Carl." The detective laughed. "Why do you like cats so?" he asked abruptly.

"Don't you?" Millicent asked.

"Yes," he said. "But it must be I like little girls better—at least, I've got five girls, and only one cat."

"A cat?" Millicent said. "You have a cat right in the house with five girls?"

"Hold it," he said. "Who's doing the questioning here? And stop answering my questions with a question of yours. Who's the detective anyway?"

"I guess I'm the criminal, so you're the detective," Millicent said.

They laughed together, but then the detective said, "Now I'd still like to know why, when no one else in your family cares much about cats at all, you love cats so much. And this time a straightforward answer."

Millicent stared, and thought. "I don't know," she answered slowly. "I've always loved them, I guess. It—it's because they're strays and they're lost. They're little! I guess that's it—they're so little to be lost. . . . I can't help it, I get all sort of soft inside when I see them." She paused. "I pick them up, and I shouldn't, because then I can't seem to put them down again—they're lost and starved, and they don't belong to anybody, and they need somebody."

"I know just what you're trying to say," the detective said promptly, "because I get that way when I pick up one of my little girls after being gone from them a whole long day. Your heart sort of gets like cheap ice cream when it melts—all watery and mushy. I guess maybe it does melt."

"Yes!" Millicent said, delighted. "Like spongy cheap ice cream," she agreed in enormous wonderment at all he knew and all he understood.

Down in the dark, Blue Angel suddenly rubbed himself against her ankles. Millicent ducked out of sight, then came up, holding the little cat for the big man to see. From behind the kitten she slowly, honestly told the detective, "I understand that a cat can't stay here—it's too awful for Mother. But when I found Blue Angel right beside my Easter basket, I got it in my mind he was a present, the biggest, best present of my whole life. Then everything went wrong. And it didn't seem fair that anything as wonderful as Blue Angel had to be taken away. Oh, I don't know how to say it better, but I still feel that way—I've got to keep Blue Angel."

"Of course, you have," the policeman agreed. "But listen, Millidollar, I don't know how we're going to manage—not yet—but at least we'll try. Your brothers and Sally should be back any minute, but you leave everything to me. All you have to do is stand where you are, but be sure to keep Blue Angel quiet. Suddenly I'll open the cabinet and pull you up, but don't you say a thing. Just look scared. That should come easy."

They laughed, and Blue Angel in Millicent's arms got excited and talked his raw-sounding miauws into their laughter.

The detective cut his laugh short. "Okay, down to business. I want to talk to your folks before I produce you out of the phonograph. Hey, there the three of them come out of the alley now!"

Without another word he shoved the cabinet door shut.

"You didn't put the garden stuff back," Millicent called out to him.

"Never mind, there isn't time. I'll stop your brothers and Sally here, then I'll call your mother down. Just think how she'll feel when I open the door and yell up to her: 'She's here, Mrs. Harding, she's here!' I'm afraid before I can get one bellow out of me those brothers of yours will come charging so hard, they'll knock me flat. . . . Keep your cat quiet!"

Detective Waters strode to the door, threw it open,

and bellowed, "Mrs. Harding! Oh, Mrs. Harding! Millicent's been found, safe and sound. Can you come down here a minute?"

He chuckled to himself. "Can she come down here a minute? Look at them all come!"

chapter nine

The Angel Club

Carl must have taken the five porch steps in one jump. As his feet crashed down and the porch shook, he yelled out, "Where is she? Where'd you find her?"

"A minute—she'll be here in a minute," the detective said from right beside the phonograph. "I'm jotting down a few notes while waiting for your mother to come down, so let's all sit on the steps and have a little family conference while we wait for Millicent. Right now all I'll tell you is that she's safe and sound."

There was a thick, disappointed silence, and they all stood still—then Mother came out on the porch. Millicent couldn't help herself, she had to see her mother, see how she was. Holding Blue Angel tight, she gentled the cabinet door open a tiny crack. The detective was leading Mother to the porch steps, and when she sat down beside Sally, he himself sat down on the topmost step. They all sat twisted about, looking up at him. He slapped his notebook shut.

"Some detective," he said. "I got so excited, I didn't get all the details, but Millicent can tell you those better than I can."

Dave and Carl looked up at the detective as if they couldn't believe their ears. He saw their disgusted look and held up his hand. "I know how you feel, but I need these few minutes, before she comes, to talk to you. Have you ever thought," he immediately began, giving them no chance to interrupt, "how it must be to be a youngest child in a family of nothing but grown-ups? In the whole household there's nothing littler than you, nothing needs you. Then there is a handy alley where there are sometimes lost cats that need you."

Millicent could see her two brothers stiffly eyeing the detective. Behind them Sally had begun to grin, and Mother looked hopefully at the man, a small smile on her face.

"All right," the detective said into their silence,

"right now you two brothers are anxious and worried, and that's how I want you, so you'll listen to me. But at the same time you're resentful too that your little sister could pull such a thoughtless, heartless stunt. And she so well brought up by her big brothers!"

Millicent peeked at Mother smiling to herself. Oh, she loved the big detective!

"Forgive me," Detective Waters was saying directly to Carl and Dave, "but I want to slam it home to you right now, before you're over your scare—as you will be, the moment I produce Millicent. Right now let's look at it, for once, from her side. How would you feel if I suddenly produced her, but told you, 'Here she is—but you can't keep her'? Yet that's what you asked of her every time she found a kitten to love in her aloneness. . . . Sure, it was for your mother's sake, but didn't that put it all up to your little sister? She must be the one always to think of your mother's allergy, and what not to do.

"But did you two men ever think of what to do? Dave, you're a dentist, Carl's going to college and wants to be a doctor, but until Millicent made this emergency for you, how often had you thought to check on new drugs? And if *I* know that over a period of time they often can desensitize people from their allergies, *you* should have known! Certainly you two well know how fast things change in the field of medicine these days."

On the step below Dave and Carl, Sally delightedly nodded along with the detective's every word, but wisely said nothing. And Mother listened hard.

The big man was quiet a moment as if to let it sink in, then without warning he slammed out the question: "Who started to make a clubhouse under the porch, and why did all of you—even you, Mrs. Harding—try to fool me? I probed and I questioned about some hideout right in the house, but none of you thought to mention the space under the porch."

"But I didn't know!" Mother said astounded.

"Nobody tried to fool you," Carl said indignantly. "We didn't think to mention it because we didn't know. So far as I know it's impossible to get under this porch, short of using a wrecking bar . . . . Hey," he interrupted himself, "if there's a way down, then it could only be through the phonograph. Millicent's under there with her cat?"

The detective nodded.

"Know why I thought of it?" Carl asked triumphantly all around. "Because as a kid I used to sit in that big phonograph. It was when Dad was chang-

ing it to a planter . . . . Is Mimi down there now?"
He jumped up and started for the phonograph, but
the detective was there first and pulled the door open.
"Okay, Millicent, come on out, but for your mother's
sake, better leave Blue Angel down there." He helped
her out and closed the cabinet. Under the porch Blue
Angel began his wails—as desperate, as forlorn, as
if he'd been forsaken for days. "Well," the detective
said above the yowls, "here then is your little sister,
and down there is the little cat, as you can hear,
already completely Millicent's. She thought he was
hers. She thought you'd given her Blue Angel for the
biggest Easter present of her whole life." He made a
sound in his throat. "And, as I could point out, Easter
isn't over yet."

They all stared at Millicent so hard it embarrassed
her. She ran to her mother, and Mother hugged her.
Dave and Carl and Sally came to stand around them
in a tight circle, as if they were never going to let her
get out of that circle again. Mother hid her face
against Millicent, said, "Mimi," and kept saying,
"Mimi." Millicent's throat began to feel terribly thick,
but she had to start explaining—they had to know
how she'd discovered the secret entrance, and what
was under the porch.

Carl nodded eagerly along with her words. Then he didn't even let her finish. "Know how I came to think of a false bottom as an entrance to get under the porch? Way back, I'd thought of it myself! I used to sit inside the cabinet while Dad was working on it. I was so-called helping him. I'd sit there pestering him to make a clubhouse for us under the porch. Sitting there, I'd got the idea that going down through its bottom would make a swell secret entrance. All us kids around that time were clubhouse crazy. We'd built a lean-to up against some kid's porch and it had come crashing down around our ears, so I was pestering Dad to make us a real clubhouse.

"Why I must have given *him* the idea. But I never knew—he never let on he was going to do it." His emotions were suddenly too much for Carl, he rubbed his nose hard, then started for the phonograph. "I've got to get down there and see."

"Me too," Dave announced, but then looked at his new suit. "Guess after backyards and alleys, it can take it," he said half apologetic, half appealing to Sally.

"Of course," Sally said. "I'm going down too."

The detective handed his flashlight to Carl. "Give me a full report—I'm too fat for phonographs."

"Oh, Carl," Millicent yammered after him. "Your flashlight is down there—broke—it won't light." It was better she told him before he found it himself.

Carl poked his head back up out of the phonograph. "That farther room is even all marked out for windows," he said. "But now I suppose besides windows, we'd want a small door—girls wouldn't want to have to go upside down through a phonograph."

"This girl does," Millicent shouted. "It's the only way, because that's the way I saved Blue Angel."

"Good for you!" Carl said delightedly. He slid down with the flashlight, with Dave and Sally right behind him.

They could hear him under the porch talking loudly over Blue Angel's questioning miauws as he exclaimed, "Golly, you *have* got blue eyes—but do you have to climb me like a tree?" Now he must be flashing the light around. "Gosh," he said. "Gosh. What this would have meant to me and the kids then! And Dad actually started this for me. Listen, Millidoll, everyone, I want to finish what he started. But a clubhouse under here—are little girls like that?"

"I am," Millicent answered him promptly. "And if Sarah isn't . . . . Mr. Waters, would your five girls come? They could bring their cat."

The detective laughed. "Except for the hemstitching one—she must be a Sarah, too—the rest of them would jump at a chance to belong to a club. But I warn you they're no angels—not even the cat."

"The Angel Club—it'll be the Angel Club," Millicent said, having decided it on the spur of that delighted moment.

Sally pulled herself up out of the phonograph. She had Blue Angel in her arms. "Phew! I'll sure have to help you scrub and decorate, Mimi, after Carl and Dave get it fixed up. No angels would go down there! But until then, I'll put Blue Angel in the car and take him home. He's yours, of course, Mimi, and you can stop to see him on your way to school and on the way back. And there'll be Saturdays and Sundays too."

Mother hugged Millicent. "And I'm going to look into what new treatments there are for allergy the first thing tomorrow. If they *do* work then your cat will live here with us."

"It's the devil's own time to be a wet blanket," Detective Waters spoke up. "But I've got to remind you—I'm still a policeman—that this is a lost cat. Better find out if anyone has advertised for him."

Millicent sagged, but Mother put an arm around her and whispered, "Mr. Waters has to be legal, but

thin and starved as Blue Angel is—even eating olives
—he's been lost a long time. You know all the back
papers stacked on the workbench—I'm sure if you go
through a month of lost-and-found ads and he isn't
there, that's legal. Why don't you go look, or there'll
be no rest?" Mother gave her a small push.

Millicent flew, but as she passed the open cupboard
in the kitchen she snatched a box of cereal to eat dry
while she sorted through all the dreary ads in the
papers downstairs. Bent over the workbench Millicent had worked her way through a month's want
ads, when the basement window suddenly pushed
open. It was Sarah. "Mill-eee, are you down here?
They said you were. Millie, I came because your
mother called this morning and from what she said
my mother thinks you ran away from home. Did you
run away from home?"

"Not from home," Millicent said through a dry
mouthful of cereal. Then she sputtered out, "Sarah,
I've got a cat, a blue cat, and his name is Blue Angel.
I didn't run away from home, because Blue Angel
came to me. And nobody's advertised so I can keep
him. Sarah—a cat with blue eyes!"

At the window Sarah shook her bemused head
until her thick eyeglasses glinted. "Blue eyes—what

won't they think of next?" Then she looked plead-
ingly at Millicent. "Millie, can I have Easter dinner
with you? You're going to have ham and I can't even
stand the smell of our goose roasting. It makes me
goose-pimply all over. Goose-pimply from roast
goose! Isn't that a good joke?"

At that moment, with Sarah still holding the window open, a banshee wail of forsaken yowls rose
from Dave's car in the drive. "Sarah," Millicent
yelped. "I know what we'll do! Why couldn't you
and I and Blue Angel have dinner at Sally's house?
Blue Angel can't be in the house with my mother
yet, but we ought to have Easter dinner with my
Easter cat."

"But cats make me squirmy," Sarah protested.

"So does goose," Millicent pointed out firmly.

Sarah looked anxious, then hopeful. "Well, maybe
a blue cat wouldn't! Imagine having dinner with a
blue cat when the pin I gave you was a blue cat too!
Isn't that funny peculiar?"

But her own idea had taken hold of Millicent. She
ignored Sarah. "Sally, oh, Sally," she called up toward the basement ceiling.

"I'm here in the car with Blue Angel, I heard you,"
Sally called back from the driveway. "I was trying to

keep him company, but he doesn't want me—he wants you . . . . It's a wonderful idea, Mimi. I'll take you and Sarah to my house right now, then when we get dinner ready I'll bring you yours and Blue Angel's too."

"Oh, I've got to get dressed," Millicent said, dithering with excitement and haste. "Do cats eat ham?" she demanded. "Oh, I know, he'll eat goose. Sarah, while I dress, you run and get Blue Angel your helping of goose for *his* Easter dinner." She stood thinking a moment. "And Blue Angel's so little, he won't eat it all. We'll take what's left to the alley!"

Sarah ran, but Millicent forced herself to take time to climb on the bench and lock the window securely.